Rockets

MOTLEY'S CREW

Captain Motley and the Pirates' Gold

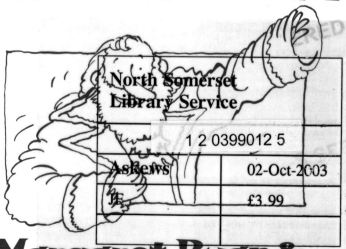

Margaret Ryan &
Margaret Chamberlain

A & C Black • London

Rockets series:

CROOK CATCHERS - Karen Wallace & Judy Brown

MOTLEY'S CREW - Margaret Ryan & Margaret Chamberlain

MR CROC - Frank Rodgers

MRS MAGIC - Wendy Smith

MY FUNNY FAMILY - Colin West

ROVER - Chris Powling & Scoular Anderson

SILLY SAUSAGE - Michaela Morgan & Dee Shulman

WIZARD'S BOY - Scoular Anderson

First paperback edition 2001
First published 2001 in hardback by
A & C Black (Publishers) Ltd
35 Bedford Row, London WC1R 4JH

Text copyright © 2001 Margaret Ryan
Illustrations copyright © 2001 Margaret Chamberlain

ISBN 0-7136-5458-9

A CIP catalogue record for this book is available
from the British Library.

Printed and bound by G. Z. Printek, Bilbao, Spain.

Chapter One

Captain Motley, of the good ship *Hesmeralda,* was sailing his boat in his bathtub when a letter arrived.

The letter fell into the soapy water. Captain Motley fished it out and opened it. It said...

SMARTEST
PIRATE SHIP
COMPETITION
In the harbour at
Deadman's Cove
next Tuesday
WIN
A HUGE BAG
of GOLD
DOUBLOONS
signed
The Chief Pirate

He got out of the bathtub and Squawk covered his eyes with his wing.

PUT ON YOUR PANTS. PUT ON YOUR HAT.

YOU CAN'T GO ON DECK LOOKING LIKE THAT.

'Oops, sorry, I forgot,' said Captain Motley, and chose his second-best pirate's uniform.

7

The crew were busy on deck. Kevin, the cabin boy, was busy reading about his comic hero, Pirate Pete.
'Why has there never been a Pirate Kev?' he wondered.

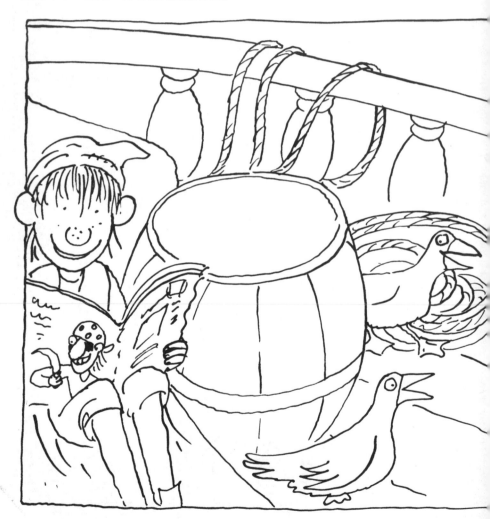

Doris McNorris, the cook, was busy
making porridge sandwiches and
singing...

'Put a sock in it, Doris,' said Smudger, the first mate. 'I'm trying to work out how much back pay the Captain owes us.'

Just then the Captain appeared on deck.

12

15

Chapter Two

To smarten up the ship, Doris did a
little light scrubbing.

To smarten up the ship, Smudger did a
little light dusting.

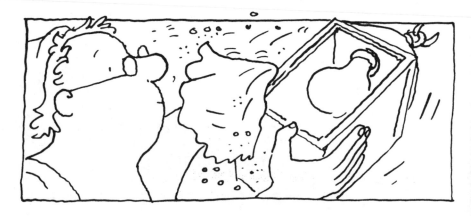

To smarten up the ship, Kevin did a
little light painting.

'Don't paint the light, dozy-head,'
yelled Smudger. 'I've just dusted that!'
'Sorry,' said Kevin and painted
the deck pink
and white
stripes instead.

By teatime the *Hesmeralda* was all ship-shape. The deck gleamed, the mast shone and the port holes had never been cleaner.

Gosh I can see out. There's a lot of sea out there...

21

While the others snored, Captain Motley took the first watch. He watched the sun go down. He watched the moon come up. He watched his eyelids go down. Then he didn't watch any more because he was fast asleep.

So he didn't see his old enemy Captain Horatio Thunderguts slip alongside in his ship, the *Saucy Stew,* and paint graffiti all over the *Hesmeralda.* Graffiti which said things like...

'What's all this?' yelled Smudger when it was his turn on watch.

Then they both heard a cackling laugh and saw outlined against the moon the ugly face of Captain Horatio Thunderguts.

Chapter Three

Next morning Captain Motley called a meeting of the crew.

Would you believe me if I told you Captain Thunderguts and his cut-throat crew sneaked on board last night, and though I fought bravely, they overpowered me, and messed up the ship?

'Fair enough,' said the Captain. 'I fell asleep. Now we'll have to paint the ship all over again.'

'We'll risk it,' said the crew.

'Second,' went on the Captain. 'We must smarten ourselves up.'

'That's what I was afraid of,' sighed the Captain. 'I'll lend you some of my clothes.'

34

Chapter Four

The day of the pirate ship competition was grey and misty. So was the *Hesmeralda*. She slipped through the mist unseen and anchored in the harbour at Deadman's Cove.

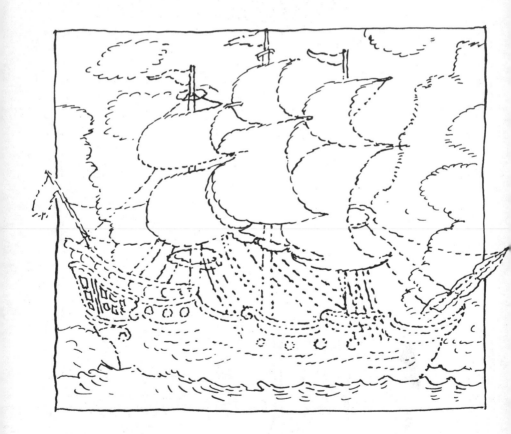

Soon the *Saucy Stew* came into view.
She was painted in every colour under
the sun.
And Captain Horatio Thunderguts was
on deck, laughing.

'I'm not,' smiled Captain Motley. 'But you soon will be. Load the porridge, Doris, and... FIRE!'

SPLUDGE!

Slimy porridge rained down on the *Saucy Stew*.

SPLODGE!

> That'll stick to your ribs.

> And your mast and your deck.

> And your nose and your ears.

The Chief Pirate was not amused when he saw the mess of the *Saucy Stew*.

And he stepped on board to inspect her.

42

'Pay at last!' grinned the crew. 'Now we can buy all the things we want.' And they went ashore to Ye Olde Pirates' Café to celebrate.

'What are you going to buy with your share of the money, Captain?' asked the crew when they had all eaten their fill of noodles, burgers, porridge and parrot food.

Captain Motley looked at his candy-striped trousers bursting at the seams, his red-and-gold coat covered in porridge and his white frilly shirt splattered with tomato ketchup.